For Marme, who taught me how to send hugs
and the importance of doing so
—HR

Acknowledgments

A very special thanks to my mom, Laurel Adam, and our dear friends Susannah Richards,
Kelly Murphy, and Antoine Revoy for so generously contributing their beautiful penmanship
to the letters featured throughout this book. And to the tireless mailpeople of the USPS,
the real Hug Delivery Specialists, who have kept us connected throughout it all.

About This Book

The illustrations for this book were done in pencil, watercolor, and digital color. This book was edited by
Alvina Ling and designed by Véronique Lefèvre Sweet. The production was supervised by Patricia Alvarado,
and the production editor was Annie McDonnell. The text was set in Kosmik OT regular, and the title type
is set in the author's hand lettering.

How to Send a HUG

Written by Hayley Rocco

Illustrated by John Rocco

LB

Little, Brown and Company ✹ New York Boston

I love hugs.
I've been told I am really good at giving them.

I can give tall hugs.

I can give short hugs.

I can even give a
Sorry, I hope you feel better hug.

But sometimes it's just not possible to give a hug.
Like the one I want to give to my grandma Gertie,
who lives so far away.

Her hugs smell like roses.

We talk on the phone a lot,
but it's just not the same.

We talk on the computer,
but even that's not the same.

Luckily, I learned how to send a hug.
Let me show you.

First, get something to write with.
This marker is my favorite.

Then find the
just-right-perfect
piece of paper.

Now you can create your hug.
You can use words or draw pictures
or even do both.

Take plenty of time,
because this is an important hug.

When you're finished,
fold it very carefully.

Your hug will be going on a long journey.

Put it in a special jacket to
keep it safe and warm.

ENVELOPES

And write on the jacket who it is going to
and where they live
so your hug doesn't get
lost along the way.

And most importantly, your hug needs a ticket for its trip.
Carefully stick its ticket in just the right spot.

There are many places where your hug can begin its journey.

It can be right in front of your house.

It can be on a street corner.

Or it can be just a slot in the wall.

Soon the Hug
Delivery Specialist
will pick it up.

They will take it to a special building where all the hugs are sorted, and their jackets are stamped so that they all end up at the right place.

Can you imagine all the hugs that go through there?

Then you have to wait while your hug completes its journey.

And wait.

And wait.

This is the hardest part.
I've been told I'm not very patient.

I like to think about all the hugs and the journeys they go on.
Some fly through the air.
Some go over waves.
And some ride past prairies, over hills, and through mountains.

Right now hugs all over the world
are being delivered by two legs

and four legs,

by four wheels

and two wheels,

by skis,

by carts,

and even by boat!

And when they arrive after
their incredible adventure,
the real magic happens....

How will you know if *your* hug arrived safely?

Because when you send a hug,

you might just get one in return.

Dear Artie,

It was so wonderful to receive your letter—thank you! I'm doing just fine over ___ ___ ___ and am so happy to hear you ___ ___ well. The roses are in full blo___ ___ ___ enclosed a photograph of a few ___ ___ ___ including the rose I ___ ___ you. There are so many butterflies ___ ___ about and I know ___ they ___ ___ to see you when ___ ___ too. I'll be sure to ___ ___ favorite chocolate chip ___ ___ arrive. Of course, we ca___ ___ ___ together, too! Mr. A___ ___ ___ favorite snuggle ___ ___ for you. ___ ___ room ___ ___ this ___ ___ shedding ___ ___ ___ knit a ___ ___ could ___ ___ you. Hel___ ___ ___ ___ tell me ___ ___ summer is ___ ___ are you su___ ___ ___ I hope ___ ___ are keeping you busy.
Love,
Grandma Gertie

Grandm...
Gertie
11 Flower St.
San Anselmo, CA

Dear Grandma Gertie,
How are you doing?
I am fine! I miss counting the butterflies
in your garden with you.
Did the roses bloom yet?
Please write
when you can.
I love you so much!!!
Love,
Artie

It may even smell like roses.

Dear Reader,

When I was little, my mother, a kindergarten teacher, helped me practice the alphabet by writing letters to family members who lived far away. Writing letters was how we stayed connected, as long-distance phone calls were very expensive. (At least that's what my mom said!)

The excitement of writing and receiving letters was a big part of my childhood. One of my uncles, who traveled quite often for work, would send postcards and letters from all over the world. I loved studying the exotic postage and could tell from the date stamp how long the letter took to arrive. These messages traveled farther than I could imagine!

When I'd leave home to visit family in California during the summer, I'd write to my best friend, who would be visiting her grandparents in New Jersey. Knowing our letters were going to be hand-delivered all the way across the United States for the cost of a twenty-five-cent stamp made it all the more exciting. We'd challenge each other to see how much we could stuff into an envelope—whether it was pictures, cutouts of movie stars, labels, or stickers. One time she sent me some clippings of her dogs' fur in a letter.

Today it is easy, quick, and pretty much free to make a phone call, send an email, or text, but the magic of writing and receiving letters has never left me. I still have letters from my grandpa that I look at from time to time. His words and drawings bring me right back to our time shared together.

I hope you can find the time to experience the same sense of magic I had when I was young, and like me, you will be able to hold on to the people who mattered in your life through the letters you shared.

Thank you for reading this book and for sharing your hugs with the people you love!

Yours truly,

Hayley